THIS WALKER BOOK BELONGS TO:

_____

_____

_____

banana

guava

orange

mango

pineapple

avocado pear

passion fruit

tangerine

banana

guava

orange

mango

pineapple

avocado pear

passion fruit

tangerine

For Emma, Linda, Nadine and Yewande

*The author would like to thank everyone
who helped her research this book,
especially Wanjiru and Nyambura
from the Kenyan Tourist Office,
and Achieng from the Kenyan High Commission.*

*The children featured in this book
are from the Luo tribe of south-west Kenya.*

First published 1994 by
Walker Books Ltd
87 Vauxhall Walk
London SE11 5HJ

This edition including DVD published 2007

4 6 8 10 9 7 5 3

© 1994 Eileen Browne

This book has been typeset in Caslon 540.

Printed in China

British Library Cataloguing in Publication Data:
a catalogue record for this book is
available from the British Library.

ISBN 978-1-4063-0749-8

www.walkerbooks.co.uk

HANDA'S SURPRISE

EILEEN BROWNE

WALKER BOOKS

AND SUBSIDIARIES

LONDON • BOSTON • SYDNEY • AUCKLAND

Handa put seven delicious fruits in a basket
for her friend, Akeyo.

She will be surprised, thought Handa
as she set off for Akeyo's village.

I wonder which fruit she'll like best?

Will she like the soft yellow banana …

or the sweet-smelling guava?

Will she like the round juicy orange …

or the ripe red mango?

Will she like the spiky-leaved pineapple …

the creamy green avocado …

or the tangy purple passion-fruit?

Which fruit will Akeyo like best?

"Hello, Akeyo," said Handa. "I've brought you a surprise."

"Tangerines!" said Akeyo. "My favourite fruit."
"TANGERINES?" said Handa. "That *is* a surprise!"

monkey

ostrich

zebra

elephant

giraffe

antelope

parrot

goat

onkey

ostrich

zebra

elephant

giraffe

antelope

parrot

goat